Diary of a Wombat

written by
Jackie French

illustrated by
Bruce Whatley

HarperCollins*Publishers*Ltd

www.harpercanada.com

HarperCollins books may be purchased for educational, business, or
sales promotional use. For information please write: Special Markets Department,
HarperCollins Canada, 2 Bloor Street East, 20th Floor, Toronto, Ontario,
Canada M4W 1A8

First published in Australia by HarperCollins Publishers Pty Ltd in 2002.
Published by arrangement with HarperCollins Publishers Pty Ltd, Sydney,
Australia.
First Canadian edition.

National Library of Canada Cataloguing in Publication

French, Jackie
Diary of a wombat / written by Jackie French; illustrated by Bruce Whatley.

ISBN 0-00-200561-1

1. Wombats – Juvenile fiction. I. Whatley, Bruce II. Title.

PZ10.3.F74Di 2003   j823'.92   C2003-901254-9

HCANZ 9 8 7 6 5 4 3 2 1

Bruce Whatley used acrylic paints to create the illustrations for this book
Cover and internal design by Lore Foye, HarperCollins Design Studio
Printed in China by Everbest Printing Co. Ltd on 128gsm Japanese Matt Art

To Mothball, and all the others.
JF

Thanks for letting me play, Jackie.
This was fun.
BW

Monday

Morning: Slept.

Afternoon: Slept.

Evening: Ate grass.

Scratched.

Night: Ate grass.

Slept.

Tuesday

Morning: Slept.

Afternoon: Slept.

Evening: Ate grass.

Night: Ate grass. Decided grass is boring.

Scratched. Hard to reach the itchy bits.

Slept.

Wednesday

Morning: Slept.

Afternoon: Mild cloudy day.

Found the perfect dustbath.

Discovered flat, hairy creature
invading my territory.

Fought major battle with
flat, hairy creature.

Won the battle.

Demanded a carrot.

The carrot was delicious.

Evening: Demanded more carrots.

No response.

Chewed hole in door.

FOR PETE'S SAKE, GIVE HER SOME CARROTS!

Ate carrots.

Scratched.

Went to sleep.

Thursday

Morning: Slept.

Afternoon:
Discovered the perfect scratching post.

Evening: Demanded carrots.
No response.
Tried yesterday's hole.
Curiously resistant to my paws.

Bashed up garbage bin
till carrots appeared.

Ate carrots.

Began new hole in soft dirt.

Went to sleep.

Friday

Morning: Slept.

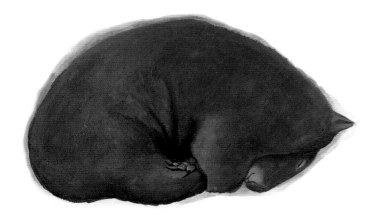

Afternoon: Discovered new scratching post.

Evening: Someone has filled in my new hole.

Soon dug it out again.

Night: Worked on hole.

Saturday

Morning: Moved into new hole.
Afternoon: Rained.

New hole filled up with water.
Moved back into old hole.

Evening: Discovered even more carrots.
Never knew there were so many carrots in the world.
Carrots delicious.

Night: Finished carrots.

Slept.

Sunday

Morning: Slept.

Afternoon: Slept.

Evening: Slept.

Night: Offered carrots at the back door.

Why would I want carrots when I feel like rolled oats?
Demanded rolled oats instead. Humans failed
to understand my simple request.
Am constantly amazed how dumb humans can be.

Chewed up one pair of boots, three cardboard boxes,
eleven flower pots and a garden chair
till they got the message.

Ate rolled oats.

Scratched. Went to sleep.

Monday

Morning: Slept.

Afternoon: Felt energetic.
Wet things flapped against
my nose on my way to the back door.

Got rid of them.

Demanded oats AND carrots.
Only had to bash the garbage bin
for five minutes before they arrived.

Evening: Have decided that humans
are easily trained and make quite good pets.

Night: Dug new hole
to be closer to them.

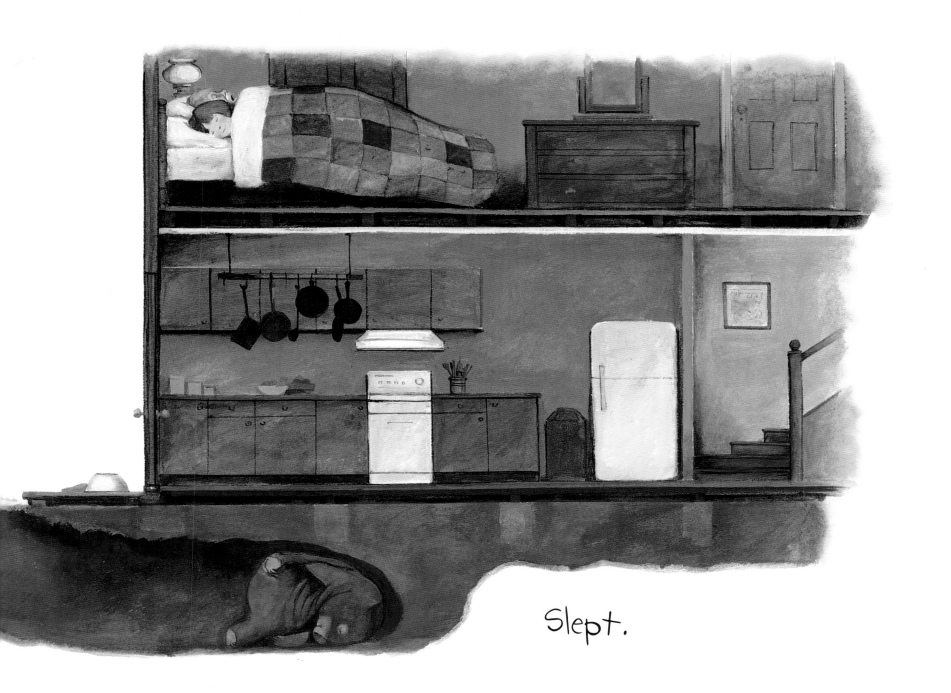

Slept.

Wombats live in Australia.
They are small, furry animals, about as big as a
medium-sized dog but with very short legs.
Wombats eat grass, but they love carrots
and rolled oats too!
They live in holes in the ground and come out
at night. (Wombats love digging holes!)
Wombats are very shortsighted. They "see"
the world with their sense of smell.